the Tanglelows

by Greg McGoon

Illustrated by Jessa Orr

Traveling the Twisting Troubling Tanglelows' Trail by Greg McGoon
Illustrations by Jessa Orr

ISBN: 978-1-938349-43-0
eISBN: 978-1-938349-44-7
Library of Congress Control Number: 2016933362

First Pelekinesis Printing 2016

For information:
Pelekinesis Publishing Group
112 Harvard Ave #65, Claremont, CA 91711 USA

www.artcentricity.org

www.pelekinesis.com

dedicated to
Olivia Parker

and all incredible teachers,

for seeing the paths that others can travel,

knowing and helping their tangles unravel.

To all of us

who find ourselves tangled from time to time,

I hope you'll connect with this playful rhyme.

To River,

Love

The
Tanglelows

Traveling the Twisting Troubling
Tanglelows' Trail

by Greg McGoon

Illustrated by Jessa Orr

Watch out for the tricky Tanglelows!

They'll find a way to fill you with WOES,

As they twist and they turn throughout your mind.

Stronger they grow, when one is unkind.

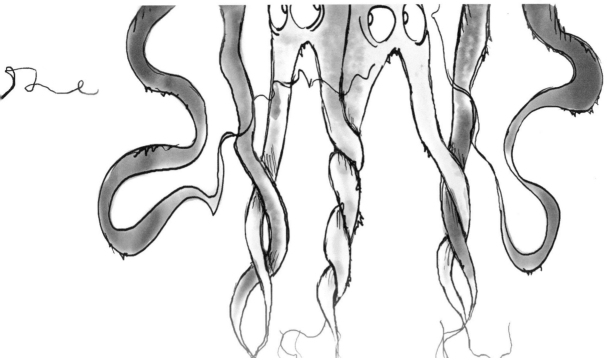

These **rascally** critters or creatures at play,
Work quickly to find their **mischievous** way,
When they hear a mean word, a sentence, or phrase,
Feel a doubt or a worry that goes **ablaze**.

They'll move in a *hurry*, and flicker and *scurry*,
It's no surprise that all will seem **blurry**.

Their sense of direction is lost, or sub par,

Till even they don't know where they are.

They'll cause your brain to be in a jumble,

Bobbing around till you feel you will fumble...

Weaving and wandering till nothing makes sense,

Making your body feel more and more tense.

Sadly, the Tanglelows lack grace and charm.
Yet to be fair they can cause you no harm.

Unless you let them sink deep in your thoughts,

Creating lots and lots of unfortunate knots.

They don't always know the trouble they cause,

It's how you respond that'll put them on pause.

Pushing or pulling only tightens their wrap,

Locking you in to this devious trap.

Then you will see the Tanglelows' maze.

A feat that surely deserves no praise,

Blocking the paths to hope and to think,

Watching your happiness surely soon shrink.

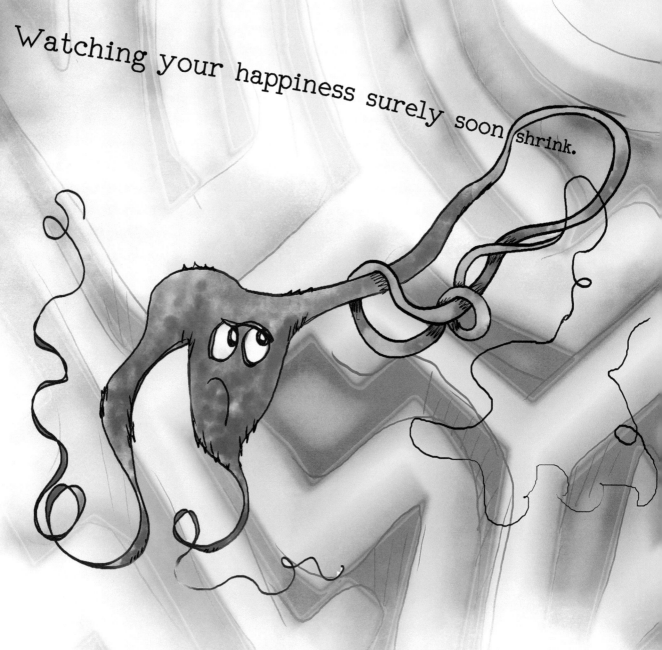

Judgment and jealousy summon them near.
Stay strong or quickly they'll lead you to...

FEAR

On a path to question all your self-worth,

Till you feel you have no place on this earth.

"What am I doing?" and "I am all wrong!"

Thoughts of "I can't!" will drag you along.

All cables crisscrossed and nothing makes sense,

How dare they build such a negative fence?"

The more they roam free within your head,

They'll feed on this clutter and further their spread.

All of your tangles with others will mingle,

In a haunting and scary and terrible jingle.

Acting out mean will widen the void;
All of yourself and others destroyed.

Adding more bricks to the Tanglelows' road,
Giving more reason for these creatures to goad.

Then you will see the Tanglelows' game!

A game that's not a matter of blame.

Blame won't mend all this troubled confusion,

As you're welcomed into a state of delusion.

How to untangle the Tanglelows' paths,
Is more than a simple problem of maths.
Untangling the tangles is a goal within reach,
You'll find it quite possible, I do beseech!

Speak to fulfill, that is a clue.
Words are not empty, be honest and true.

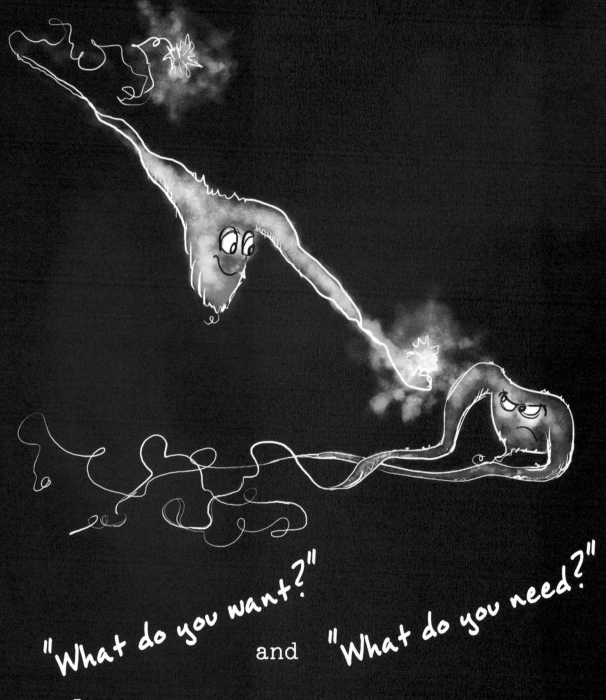

"What do you want?" and "What do you need?"
A lesson they ask for you to take heed.

It's more than speaking of wishes and dreams.

It's building belief and action, it seems.

Love what **you** love, live who **you** are!

That is a life for you to go far.

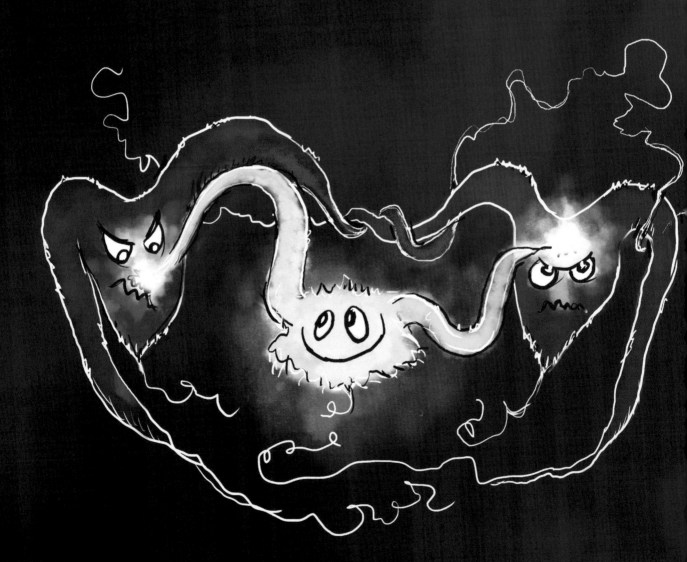

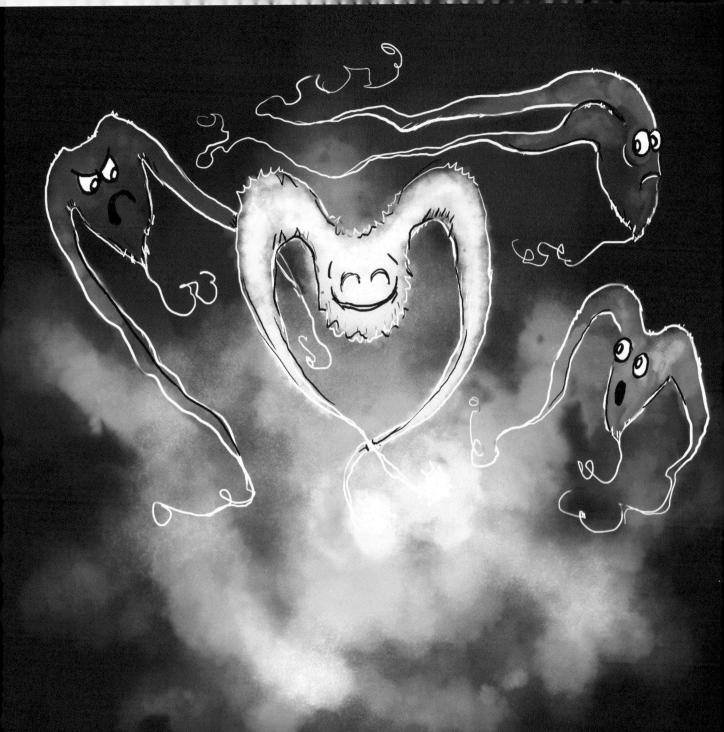

Open your heart to the beauty of you,

That is a way for all to take cue.

The greatest gift for you to give back,

with focus and patience and kindness to pack.

Your truth may feel small,

but is most solid of all:

A burden you think,

but a blessing to haul.

The stronger it grows,

the lighter the load,

Unwinding

the

tangles,

Unblocking

the

road!

It may not be easy; it may be a task,

"What is the point?" you simply might ask.

That is the beauty for you to discover.

"What is the first thing you will uncover?"

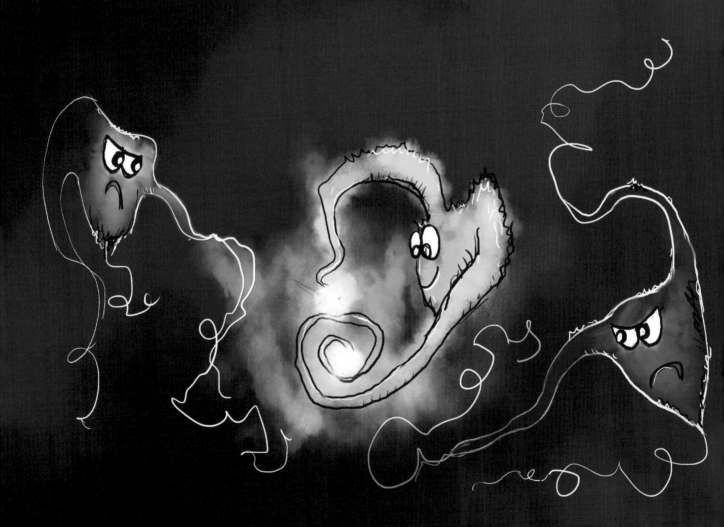

If ever you've laughed, remember you can.

It will happen again, that's part of the plan!

Now find your way to laugh and to smile.

That is a challenge not nearly as vile.

No matter the manner they cause you to feel,

There's certainly hope that you will heal.

Out of the chaos with nothing to prove,

Be free to continue to carve your own groove.

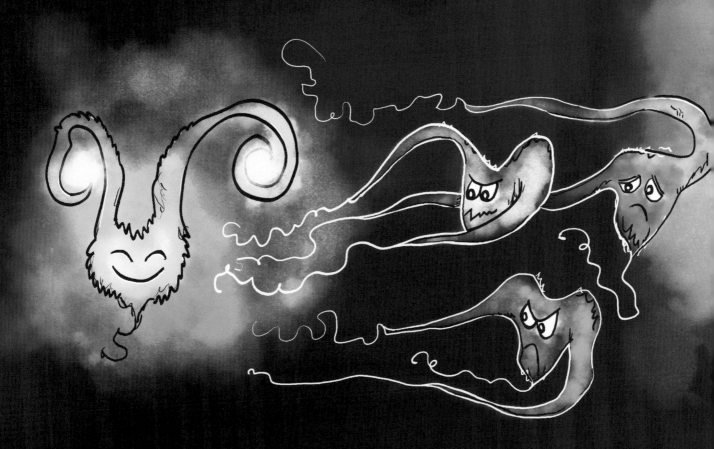

Connect with yourself and these creatures will see,

Building that bond will cause them to flee.

And so to unwind the Tanglelows' trail,

Take a deep breath, it's time to set sail.

As days go by with highs and lows,
Remember the bumbling Tanglelows,
Creeping their way to and fro,
Creating a mess wherever they go.

Now, even the toughest of tangles, the hardest to crack,
A love for yourself can keep you on track.
So, goodbye to the Tanglelows' trench of delusion,
Your visit for now has reached its conclusion.

But, watch out for the tricky Tanglelows.
They'll find a way to fill you with woes,
As they twist and turn throughout your mind.
Stronger they grow, if one is unkind.

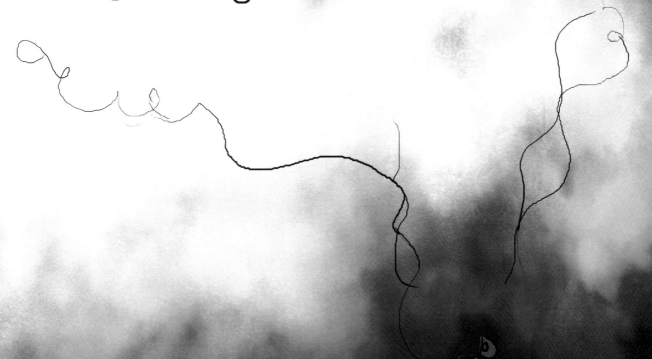

CPSIA information can be obtained at www.ICGtesting.com
Printed in the USA
BVIW12n2223250216
438021BV00001B/2

* 9 7 8 1 9 3 8 3 4 9 4 3 0 *